Caring for Your
Potbellied Pig

Leia Tait

Weigl Publishers Inc.

Project Coordinator
Heather C. Hudak

Design
Warren Clark

Published by Weigl Publishers Inc.
350 5th Avenue, Suite 3304, PMB 6G
New York, NY 10118-0069
Web site: www.weigl.com

Library of Congress Cataloging-in-Publication Data

Tait, Leia.
  Caring for your potbellied pig / by Leia Tait.
     p. cm. -- (Caring for your pet)
  Includes index.
  ISBN 1-59036-474-0 (library binding : alk. paper) -- ISBN 1-59036-475-9 (soft cover : alk. paper)
  1. Potbellied pigs as pets--Juvenile literature. I. Title. II. Series: Caring for your pet (Mankato, Minn.)
  SF393.P74T35 2007
  636.4'85--dc22

                              2006016103

                    Printed in the United States of America
                    1 2 3 4 5 6 7 8 9 0   10 09 08 07 06

Locate the pig hoof prints throughout the book to find useful tips on caring for your pet.

Photograph and Text Credits
Every reasonable effort has been made to trace ownership and to obtain permission to reprint copyright material. The publishers would be pleased to have any errors or omissions brought to their attention so that they may be corrected in subsequent printings.

Darlene Duvall and Harley: pages 10 top, 21; **Morris Farm:** pages 6 right, 10 bottom; **Moorpark College Zoo:** page 7 left.

Cover: Potbellied pigs make smart, friendly pets.

All of the Internet URLs given in the book were valid at the time of publication. However, due to the dynamic nature of the Internet, some addresses may have changed, or sites may have ceased to exist since publication. While the author and publisher regret any inconvenience this may cause readers, no responsibility for any such changes can be accepted by either the author or the publisher.

Contents

Potbellied Pals

Pigs are interesting animals. They are curious and playful. Pigs are one of the smartest tame animals, and they are easy to train. Many people in North America think of pigs only as **livestock**. However, in the past 30 years, pigs have become popular pets. Although some people keep farm pigs as pets, most people choose **miniature** pigs. There are many different types of miniature pigs, but the most popular is the potbellied pig.

Potbellied pigs have hair instead of fur. This makes them a good pet for people with allergies.

Some pet owners enjoy dressing up their potbellied pigs for special occasions.

Potbellied pigs are also called Vietnamese or Chinese pigs. They make excellent pets. They are smart, friendly, affectionate, and they learn quickly. Unlike many common pets, potbellied pigs shed very little hair. They also do not bark, smell, carry fleas, or cause **allergies** to act up. Even though they are miniature, potbellied pigs are a big responsibility for pet owners. They need to be fed, groomed, and exercised every day. At times, they can misbehave, so you must pay extra attention to your potbellied pig.

■ Like people, potbellied pigs need a diet that is high in fiber.

Fascinating Facts

- March 1 is National Pig Day in the United States. It is a day for celebrating the intelligence and usefulness of pigs.
- Potbellied pigs have excellent memories. They do not forget what they learn.
- There are more than 11.6 million pigs in Vietnam.
- The pig is the fifth-smartest animal in the world. Only humans, apes, dolphins, and whales are smarter.

Pet Profiles

Potbellied pigs are one **breed** of miniature pig. Miniature pigs are about one eighth the size of ordinary farm pigs, which can weigh more than 1,000 pounds (454 kilograms). Most miniature pigs weigh between 60 and 175 pounds (27 and 79 kg). There are more than 30 different **varieties** of miniature pigs in the world today.

POTBELLIED OR VIETNAMESE

- Dwarf
- Originally from Asia
- **Swayed** back and large, sagging belly
- Short, upright ears
- Straight tail with a tuft of hair on the tip
- Black, white, or black-and-white
- Weighs 30 to 150 pounds (14 to 68 kg)
- Friendly and affectionate

JULIANI OR PAINTED MINI

- Dwarf
- Originally from Europe
- Swayed back and slightly oversized belly
- Small to medium ears
- Short, straight tail
- Multicolored, including red, black, white, or silver
- Weighs 15 to 60 pounds (7 to 27 kg)
- Gentle, playful nature
- Short hair

AFRICAN PYGMY OR GUINEA HOG

- Midget
- Originally from Africa
- Straight back and stomach
- Medium, upright ears
- Kinked tail
- Shiny, black coat with white markings
- Bristly hair
- Weighs 30 to 60 pounds (14 to 27 kg)
- Active and energetic

All miniature pigs are either midgets or dwarfs. A midget looks the same as a livestock pig, except it is much smaller. Dwarf pigs have shorter legs than an ordinary pig. However, the head and body of a dwarf pig may be large in comparison to the rest of its body. Unlike livestock pigs, miniature pigs often have a straight tail similar to those of wild pigs.

YUCATAN OR MEXICAN HAIRLESS

- Dwarf
- Originally from Mexico and Central America
- Straight back and stomach
- Medium-sized ears
- Dark gray or black with little to no hair
- Stands 16 to 24 inches (41 to 61 centimeters) tall
- Weighs 50 to 100 pounds (23 to 46 kg)
- Gentle nature

OSSABAW ISLAND

- Dwarf
- Lives wild on Ossabaw Island, off the southeast coast of the United States
- Straight back and stomach
- Short, upright ears
- Straight tail
- Multicolored
- Weighs 25 to 90 pounds (11 to 41 kg)
- Lively and friendly
- Heavy coat

Learn as much as you can about miniature pigs before deciding to choose one for a pet.

Hog History

Pigs belong to the *Sus scrofa* **species**. All domestic pigs today come from wild boars that first roamed ancient Europe and Asia 36 million, years ago. Over time, early pigs developed into a number of different breeds. Scientists believe that **ancestors** of the potbellied breed lived as many as 4 million years ago in Southeast Asia and China. People first tamed pigs in these countries about 7,000 years ago. Potbellied pigs became popular as both farm animals and pets.

■ Today, wild boars live in the woodlands of Europe, Asia, and northern Africa.

In the 1950s, potbellied pigs were sent to Europe as zoo animals. In 1985, a Canadian zoo director named Keith Connell saw potbellied pigs on display in Europe. He became interested in these unusual animals and brought 18 of them to Canada. These were the first potbellied pigs in North America. Connell wanted to sell the pigs to zoos. Instead, people bought the pigs as pets. They quickly became very popular.

In 1989, a man named Keith Leavitt brought several potbellied pigs into the United States. Today, there are more than 200,000 potbellied pigs in North America. Most are related to the pigs first brought to North America by Connell and Leavitt.

To register your potbellied pig in North America, she must be descended from either the Connell or Leavitt lines.

■ A bronze pig is one of 12 animal sculptures that decorate the Old Summer Palace in China. The palace was built during the Qing Dynasty.

Fascinating Facts

- The oldest drawing of a pig was painted on a cave wall in Spain. The drawing is more than 40,000 years old.
- At least 457 million pigs live in China today.
- More potbellied pigs live in the United States than in any other country.

Life Cycle

Potbellied pigs live for about 20 years. They change as they grow. As a pet owner, it is important to know the different stages of your pig's life. The more you understand about these stages, the better you will be able to care for your pet pig.

Newborn

Baby pigs are called piglets. Potbellied piglets grow inside their mothers for nearly four months. Newborn piglets weigh between 4 and 8 ounces (113 and 227 grams). They are very delicate when they are born. During the first weeks of their life, piglets spend most of their time drinking their mothers' milk and getting to know the world around them.

One Year and Up

After one year of age, potbellied pigs grow more slowly. By the time they are 2 years old, potbellied pigs are fully grown. They will continue to gain weight for at least another year. Potbellied pigs reach their full, adult size between 3 and 4 years of age. The average full-grown potbellied pig is 16 inches (41 cm) tall and weighs 100 pounds (45 kg). Females are bigger than males, and they grow larger with every litter they produce.

Fascinating Facts

- The most piglets ever born in a single **litter** was 37.
- Pigs enjoy a routine. They like to return to familiar places, such as mud holes, **salt licks**, and **rooting** grounds.

Five to Eight Weeks

At around 5 weeks, piglets begin eating solid foods and stop drinking milk from their mothers. At this age, they grow quickly. Potbellied piglets should stay with their mother and littermates until they are at least 6 or 7 weeks old. They should not be adopted as pets before this time.

Six Months

At about 6 months of age, potbellied pigs begin to mature. Their baby teeth fall out and are replaced by permanent, adult teeth. Although their body is not finished growing, pigs can begin having babies of their own. Mother pigs, called sows, can have one or two litters each year. There are usually about six piglets in each litter. Some sows have as many as 14 piglets at one time.

Picking Your Pet

It is easy to fall in love with the cute face and intelligence of a potbellied pig. However, there are many things to consider before choosing a potbellied pig as a pet. A pet pig could be part of your family for 20 years. Consider the following questions to help you decide if a potbellied pig is the right pet for you.

Potbellied pigs are not allowed to be kept as pets in some communities, towns, and cities.

Are Potbellied Pigs Allowed as Pets Where I Live?

Before deciding on a pet pig, find out whether the laws in your area allow potbellied pigs to be kept as pets. Some communities consider miniature pigs to be farm animals. Others have restrictions, or limits, based on the size of your yard. Some laws require that the pig be registered. Contact the local city hall or animal control organization to find out if your community has rules about keeping pigs as pets.

■ Some cities do not allow livestock or farm animals to be kept as pets. However, they may still allow potbellied pigs.

How Do I Purchase a Potbellied Pig?

It is always best to buy a pet pig from a **breeder**. A breeder can provide supplies and information about the pig. Most importantly, a breeder should be able to provide proof that your pig is a **purebred** potbelly. This is important, since a pig that is not purebred could grow as large as 600 pounds (272 kg). To be certain that the pig is purebred, ask for registration papers. To find a reliable breeder in your area, contact a local **veterinarian**, pig club, or the North American Potbellied Pig Association.

■ A reliable breeder will show you many different potbellied pigs.

Is My Home Suitable for a Potbellied Pig?

A pet pig will need an outdoor area where she can exercise and root around in the ground. This space should be fenced in to prevent the pig from escaping and to protect her from neighborhood dogs. A pet pig will also need an indoor space large enough for a bed, food and water dishes, and a litter box.

Fascinating Facts

- Potbellied pigs often can be adopted from animal rescue agencies. Most of these pigs are full-grown and trained to be pets. Some of these pigs come from pet owners who could no longer care for their pet. Others have been rescued from homes where they were mistreated.
- Most purebred potbellied pigs cost about the same amount as a purebred dog. The largest amount of money ever paid for a potbellied pig was $37,000.

Pig Supplies

Moving to a new home is stressful. To help a potbellied pig adjust to her new setting, have a special space ready before bringing her home. Some supplies your pig will need include food and water dishes, a bed, a harness and leash, and toys. The dishes should be heavy so they do not tip over when the pig nudges them with her snout.

Your pig also will need a litter box. This can be made from almost any kind of box. Make sure that the box is big enough for your pig to turn around inside. The box should have a low opening—no higher than 3 inches (8 cm)—so the pig can enter and exit easily. Line the litter box with newspapers or cedar woodchips. Do not put the litter box near the pig's eating area. Pigs are clean animals and do not like to eat near their litter box.

Never use cat litter in a pig's litter box. Pigs will sometimes eat it.

■ To walk a pet pig, purchase a loose-fitting harness made from a soft material.

Your potbellied pig will need a bed to sleep in at night and rest in during the day. A large dog bed or crate works well. Line the bed with soft material, such as old comforters or sleeping bags, that the pig can use to burrow into. Keep the bed in a quiet, warm part of your house, away from drafts. Very young piglets like to cuddle up to something warm in their beds. This reminds them of their mother and littermates, so they feel safe. When you first bring a piglet home, fill a hot water bottle with warm water and wrap it in a towel. Place it in your pet's bed. Do this for a few weeks, while your pig adjusts to your home.

■■■ Having some simple supplies, such as a hot water bottle and litter box, ready before bringing a pig home will make the experience much more comfortable for your pet.

Fascinating Facts

- Some pigs have trouble climbing. Your pet may need a ramp to help her up and down stairs.
- Pigs need regular exercise to stay healthy. Potbellied pigs can be trained to wear a harness and leash for daily walks outside.

Miniature Munchies

All pigs love to eat. They will eat just about anything, even if they are not hungry. You will need to control your pig's diet to make sure he does not become overweight. Never feed a potbellied pig food that is meant for farm pigs. This type of food will not provide the **nutrients** he needs to stay healthy. Instead, feed your pet food made just for miniature pigs. You can buy special potbellied pig food from your breeder or your local pet store. Be sure to store the food in an airtight container to keep it fresh.

Never underfeed a pig to try to control her weight. Underfeeding will make her weak and ill.

■ A pet pig should have a daily serving of leafy green vegetables.

Fascinating Facts

- All pigs are omnivores. They eat both plants and meat.
- Pigs cannot tell when they have had enough to eat. They will eat until there is nothing left in their dish.
- Papaya is especially good for potbellied pigs. It is high in vitamins A and C. Another part of papaya, called papain, will naturally freshen a pig's breath.

Potbellied piglets under 3 months of age can eat as much as they want. Pigs older than 3 months need 1.5 to 2 cups (355 and 473 milliliters) of food each day. Feed your pig twice each day—once in the morning and once in the evening. To get all the proper nutrients, a potbellied pig should eat a variety of foods. As an afternoon snack, a pig can eat a salad of fresh vegetables, such as lettuce, celery, carrots, and peas. Sometimes, you can give your pig a fresh fruit snack, such as apples, bananas, grapes, watermelon rinds, oranges, raisins, or melon. Never feed your pig corn, cheese, meat, chocolate, table scraps, or food made for other animals. Make sure your potbellied pig has fresh, clean water at all times, too.

■ To prevent pet pigs from eating too much sugar, their diets should contain three times more vegetables than fruits.

Potbellied Bodies

Potbellied pigs have interesting bodies. Their back, stomach, and face look quite different from farm pigs. Other parts of their body are common to all pigs. People have bred potbellied pigs to have certain **traits**. Other traits have developed naturally over time.

A potbellied pig's skin is th
It is covered with bristly ha
which they shed once or tw
each year. Pigs have very fe
sweat **glands**, which make
difficult for them to keep c

Potbellied pigs have a swayed back. This causes their large belly to hang near the ground.

A potbellied pig has a straight tail that has a tuft of hair at the tip.

▬ POTBELLIED PIG

Potbellied pigs have a big, round stomach. At times, the potbellied pig's stomach can be so large that it drags along the ground.

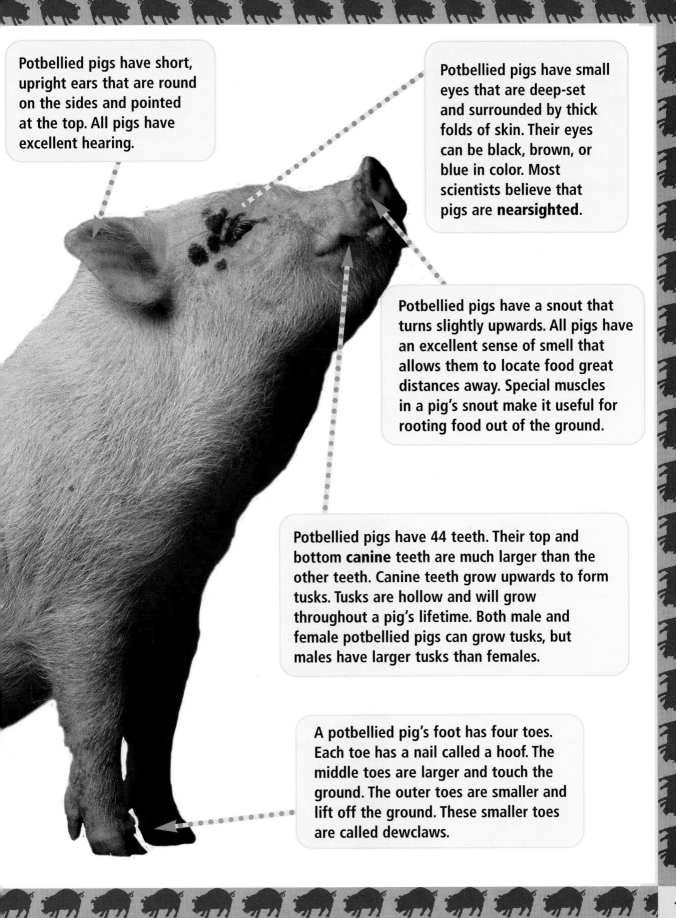

Potbellied pigs have short, upright ears that are round on the sides and pointed at the top. All pigs have excellent hearing.

Potbellied pigs have small eyes that are deep-set and surrounded by thick folds of skin. Their eyes can be black, brown, or blue in color. Most scientists believe that pigs are **nearsighted**.

Potbellied pigs have a snout that turns slightly upwards. All pigs have an excellent sense of smell that allows them to locate food great distances away. Special muscles in a pig's snout make it useful for rooting food out of the ground.

Potbellied pigs have 44 teeth. Their top and bottom **canine** teeth are much larger than the other teeth. Canine teeth grow upwards to form tusks. Tusks are hollow and will grow throughout a pig's lifetime. Both male and female potbellied pigs can grow tusks, but males have larger tusks than females.

A potbellied pig's foot has four toes. Each toe has a nail called a hoof. The middle toes are larger and touch the ground. The outer toes are smaller and lift off the ground. These smaller toes are called dewclaws.

Perfect Pigs

Pet pigs enjoy regular grooming. Despite their reputation for loving mud, pigs are one of the cleanest animals on the planet. They like to be as clean as possible.

Clean your pig's teeth with a washcloth and baking soda a few times each week. Use another damp, warm cloth to wipe around the pig's eyes. Once a month, clean the pig's ears, too. Grooming should also include a trip to the veterinarian to trim the pig's hooves and tusks. Hooves that are too long can cause leg and joint problems. Sharp tusks may also cause the pig to accidentally injure herself, you, or your other pets.

Never use perfume, oil, or other products made for humans on a potbellied pig.

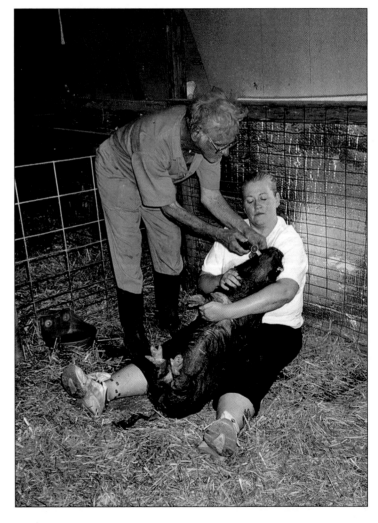

■ During tusk trimming, it is a good idea to lay the pig comfortably on her back. Talk to her in a low voice and rub her tummy to help her feel safe.

A potbellied pig's skin needs to be kept clean. This will prevent **parasites**, such as worms or mites. Brush the pig's skin in a gentle, circular motion to remove dead hair and flakes. If the pig is very dirty, she may need a bath. Since pigs are naturally clean animals, this should be done only when necessary, and no more than once every 6 weeks. Potbellied pigs have dry skin. Use special shampoos and moisturizers made just for pigs. Feeding a pig foods that are high in Vitamin E, such as avocados and banana leaves, will also help improve her skin.

■ If cared for properly, most potbellied pigs will live longer than dogs.

Fascinating Facts

- If your pig is nervous about having a bath, float some toasted oats cereal on the surface of the water as a treat to keep her occupied.
- Potbellied pigs' skin is easily sunburned. Apply sun block to prevent sunburn.

Healthy and Happy

Soon after you bring home your potbellied pig, he will need to visit a veterinarian. The veterinarian will check your new pet's health, look for signs of illness, and give him **vaccinations**. The pig will need to return to the veterinarian for regular check-ups at least once a year. He may also need treatment if he becomes ill. Potbellied pigs can become ill from parasites or from infections caused by cuts that are not cleaned properly. They can also catch diseases from other pigs or humans.

While your pig is young, touch him all over. This will make trips to the veterinarian less stressful, as he will be comfortable being examined.

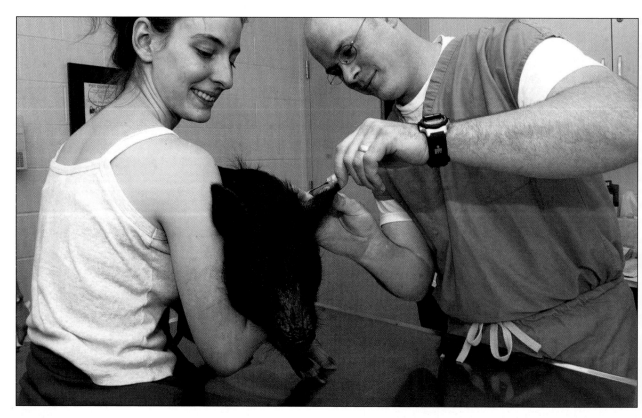

■ Veterinarians may plant a computer chip in a pet pig's ear. The chip stores information about the pig's owner.

A potbellied pig can also become ill from extreme heat or cold. If your pig becomes wet from rain or snow, quickly and thoroughly dry him, or he may catch a cold. In summer, provide your pig with shade and cool, clean water where she can wade.

It is important to notice when a pig is not feeling well. Signs that a pig is sick include fever or trouble breathing. If the pig stops eating or will not get up from lying down, something is wrong. Take the pig to the veterinarian if you see any of these signs or notice other sudden changes in the pig's behavior.

A child's plastic wading pool is a good way to keep your potbellied pig cool on warm days.

Fascinating Facts

- Diseases passed between animals and people are called zoonoses. These diseases can be passed on by touching the skin of an infected person or animal, breathing in germs, or eating infected foods. To avoid zoonoses, practice good **hygiene**.
- Not all veterinarians know how to treat potbellied pigs. You may need to search for a veterinarian who has studied these interesting animals.

Playing with Pigs

Wild pigs live in groups called herds. They naturally create a "pecking order." This means that each pig has a place in the herd. One pig is the boss. Your pet pig will begin testing your rules to find out where she fits in your home's pecking order. She will try to be the boss. You must make it clear that you are in charge. If you do not, the pig will become spoiled and demanding.

Teaching a pig to be well behaved takes time. The best way to train a pig is to reward her for good behavior. Giving her a small bit of food, such as a raisin, is a good reward.

Pigs have a great deal of energy and love to play. They are smart, so they will become bored if they are not kept busy. Teaching a pig some tricks will keep her occupied and provide her with exercise.

During training, never try to force the pig to do a trick or activity. She will become upset.

▬ Pigs love a good scratch behind the ear.

Pet Peeves

Potbellied pigs do not like:
- rough treatment
- being chased
- temperatures that are too hot or too cold
- messy living areas
- litter boxes near their food
- being thirsty

Spend about 15 minutes each day teaching your pet new tricks. You can train a pig to sit, kneel, dance, twirl, or jump through a hoop. Your pig will love to play with you. Make up games to play with her. Show your pig affection by scratching her back and rubbing her tummy.

Potbellied pigs like to play with toys. Toys made for children under 18 months of age are best. You can also provide a pig with plastic buckets, milk jugs, or cardboard boxes. She will chase, chew, tug, and root around these items for hours.

■ On National Pig Day in the United States, many pet pig owners put on shows displaying their pets' unique talents.

Fascinating Facts

- Potbellied pigs grunt, squeal, and snort to express their feelings. They also respond to similar sounds from humans, so practice talking to your pig.
- Just like dogs, potbellied pigs like to play fetch. Throw a ball, a knotted sock, or a special toy during playtime.
- Pigs can swim. Coax your pig into the water with a treat and watch her have some fun. Always stay near your pig so you can help if she becomes tired. Never throw your pig into the water or leave her unattended.

Swine Stories

In Europe, South America, and the United States, the police train potbellied pigs to sniff out illegal substances. While dogs are the most common animals for this task, potbellied pigs have proven to be better at it. Pigs are also less expensive to train.

Other potbellied pigs act as companions for people who are sick, lonely, or in need of affection. With their owners, they travel to hospitals and nursing homes. They visit with patients and perform tricks. Potbellied pigs can be very sensitive to human feelings. They can tell when someone is sad or lonely.

Throughout history, the pig has been featured in some cultures' religious beliefs. In ancient Egypt, the sky-goddess Nut sometimes appeared as a sow. Similarly, the Hindu god Vishnu is believed to transform into a giant boar. Ancient Greeks also associated pigs with Demeter, the goddess of farming.

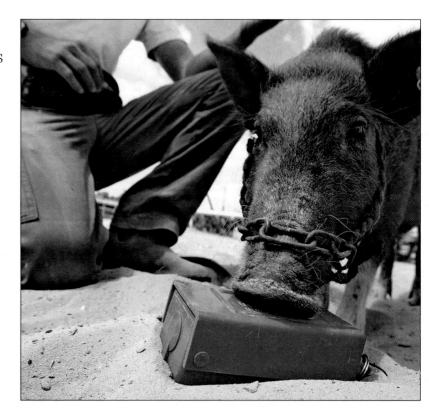

■ Miniature pigs have been trained by the Israeli army to sniff out bombs and other explosive materials.

Fascinating Facts

- An ancient name for Ireland was *Muic-inis*, or "Pig Island."
- In medieval Britain, peasants used pigs instead of dogs for hunting.

In Asia, people have long thought of pigs as special animals. The pig was a symbol of wealth 900 years ago in China. When people died, a pig was buried with them as a sign of respect. If people could not afford to own pigs, they made a clay pig to place in the grave. This pig was filled with money to show respect to the person who had passed away. Some people believe that this tradition was the beginning of the modern-day piggy bank. Today, the pig remains a symbol of good luck in China.

■ The term "piggy bank" may have came from Great Britain, where money jars were made from a clay called "pygg."

The Camel and the Pig

This Hindu folk tale shows that being different can be a good thing.

One day a camel said, "Nothing like being tall! See how tall I am!"

Hearing this, a nearby pig said, "Nothing like being short! See how short I am!"

The camel told the pig that he would prove being tall was better than being short. If he failed, the camel would give up his hump. The pig said he would prove that being short was better or give up his snout.

The pig and the camel walked toward a garden. A low wall enclosed the garden. The camel reached his long neck over the wall to eat the garden plants. Then camel turned to the pig and said, "Now, would you rather be tall or short?"

The pig was silent. The two continued walking. Soon, they came to a garden that was enclosed by a high wall with a gate at one end. The pig entered the garden through the gate. He ate his fill of vegetables. The pig laughed at the camel, who was too tall to enter the garden through the gate. The pig said to the camel, "Now, would you be tall or short?"

Together, the pig and the camel thought the matter over. They decided that the camel should keep his hump and the pig should keep his snout. The pair had learned that sometimes being tall is better, and other times being short is better.

Pet Puzzlers

What have you learned about potbellied pigs? If you can answer these questions correctly, you may be ready to own a pet pig.

Q Where are potbellied pigs originally from?

Potbellied pigs are originally from Southeast Asia and China.

Q What are the two types of miniature pigs?

Miniature pigs can be midgets or dwarfs.

Q How long have pigs been wandering Earth?

Pigs have been wandering Earth for 36 million years.

Q When did potbellied pigs first arrive in North America?

Potbellied pigs were first brought to North America in 1985.

Q How long do potbellied sows carry their babies before giving birth?

Potbellied sows carry their young for about four months.

Q What are the two small toes on each of a pig's feet called?

The two small toes on each of a pig's feet are called dewclaws.

Q What two jobs do potbellied pigs sometimes have?

Potbellied pigs sometimes sniff out illegal substances and act as companion animals.

Hog Handles

Before your buy your pet potbellied pig, write down some pig names that you like. Some names may work better for a female pig. Others may suit a male pig. Here are a few suggestions.

Bebop

Daisy

Lola

Spike

Hampton

Buttercup

Petunia

Wilbur

Hamlet

Frequently Asked Questions

What is the best way to handle a pet pig?

To handle your pig, cup one arm under his chest and the other under his rump. Gently cradle the pig against your body so he cannot wriggle free. Be careful your pig does not fall and injure himself. Make him feel secure by gently cupping your hand over his snout.

Do potbellied pigs get along well with other animals?

Potbellied pigs are very friendly. Most love to interact with other animals and people. Always introduce your pig to other pets slowly. Give the animals time to adjust to each other. Pigs and cats almost always get along. Dogs and pigs usually get along well. However, dogs are the natural **predators** of pigs. Never leave a pig alone with a dog.

How can I tell if my potbellied pig is overweight?

Pigs are naturally slim animals. You should be able to feel your pet's hip bones and ribs but not see them. If you have to search for the pig's bones through a layer of fat, he is overweight. If you can see his ribs, increase his daily amount of food.

More Information

Animal Organizations

You can help potbellied pigs stay happy and healthy by learning more about them. Many organizations are dedicated to teaching people how to care for and protect their potbellied pets. For more potbellied pig information, contact the following organizations:

North American Potbellied Pig Association (NAPPA)
3850 Dacy Lane
Kyle, TX 78640

International Potbellied Pig Registry
c/o Carolyn Kurela, Registrar
43 Quenby Mountain Road
Great Meadows, N.J. 07838

Websites

To answer more of your pig questions, visit the following websites:

North American Potbellied Pig Association (NAPPA)
www.petpigs.com

Animals for Awareness
www.animalsforawareness.org/cs_pigs.php

Words to Know

allergies: sensitivities to items, causing breathing difficulties and skin rash

ancestors: members of a family who lived long ago

breed: different types of animals

breeder: a person who raises animals and sells them

canine: large, pointed teeth in the upper and lower jaws

glands: body parts that release substances such as hormones and sweat

hygiene: clean and healthy habits

litter: babies born at the same time to one mother

livestock: animals raised for food

miniature: smaller than average

nearsighted: unable to see distant objects clearly

nutrients: vitamins and minerals in food

parasites: living things that live on or in the bodies of other animals

predators: animals that hunt and kill other animals for food

purebred: an animal whose parents are known and have qualities that have been passed on for generations

register: to fill out papers that prove an animal is purebred

rooting: digging with the snout or nose

salt licks: blocks of salt that animals lick

species: a group of living things that share certain features

swayed: to have a downward curve

traits: qualities of an animal

vaccinations: medicines that help prevent certain diseases

varieties: animals that have unique traits

veterinarian: an animal doctor

Index